SARAH

PLAYBILL

OPERA

FLYNN
THEATER
PARKING
7639401

ADMIT
ONE
OPERA
8.00
ROW
SEAT
STUB

For Sam. For Ella.
Thanks for all the squeezy hugs and noisy kisses!
R. H. H.

For my big sister, Rachel.
H. B.

First Candlewick Press edition 2004

Library of Congress Cataloging-in-Publication Data
Harris, Robie H.
Don't forget to come back! / Robie H. Harris : pictures by Harry Bliss. — 1st ed.
p. cm.
Summary: When her parents go out for the evening, a little girl threatens to run off
to the South Pole but has a good time with the babysitter instead.
ISBN 0-7636-1782-2
[1. Babysitters — Fiction.] I. Bliss, Harry, date, ill. II. Title.
PZ7.H2436 Do 2004
[E] — dc21   2002074169

2 4 6 8 10 9 7 5 3 1

Printed in China

This book was typeset in Alghera.
The illustrations were done in watercolor and ink.

Candlewick Press
2067 Massachusetts Avenue
Cambridge, Massachusetts 02140

visit us at www.candlewick.com

Don't Forget to Come Back!

Robie H. Harris

pictures by Harry Bliss

CANDLEWICK PRESS
CAMBRIDGE, MASSACHUSETTS

Guess what?
Yesterday Daddy told me something very
important. He told me that he and Mommy
were going out right after supper—and
Sarah was coming to babysit.

I didn't like that one bit!

So I told Daddy three very
important things.

I still wanted Daddy and Mommy to stay home with me. So I told Daddy three very scary things.

"1. If you go out tonight, the most giant, most loudest thunderstorm ever will come — and blow our house down!

"2. If you go out tonight, I'll get a very bad tummy ache — and I'll throw up!

"3. And if you go out tonight, the biggest baddest moose will walk into the kitchen — and eat me all up!"

That didn't scare Daddy at all!

I ran and grabbed Panda, a bag of chips,
my bike helmet, my monster book, my ballet shoes,
my umbrella, and my toothbrush.

See, I'm ready to go. And if you really, really love me, you'll take me with you.
We always love you, Pumpkin, even when we go out.

Daddy always calls me Sugar and Mommy always calls me Pumpkin just before they go out. So the bad news was — they were still going out.

I know what to do! Mommy, you go out. Daddy can stay with me. And we won't need Sarah.

Don't worry, Pumpkin. We won't be gone for long.

Well, if you go out, I won't be nice anymore. And you won't like that!

I was so-ooo mad,
I ran into the closet
and shut the door.

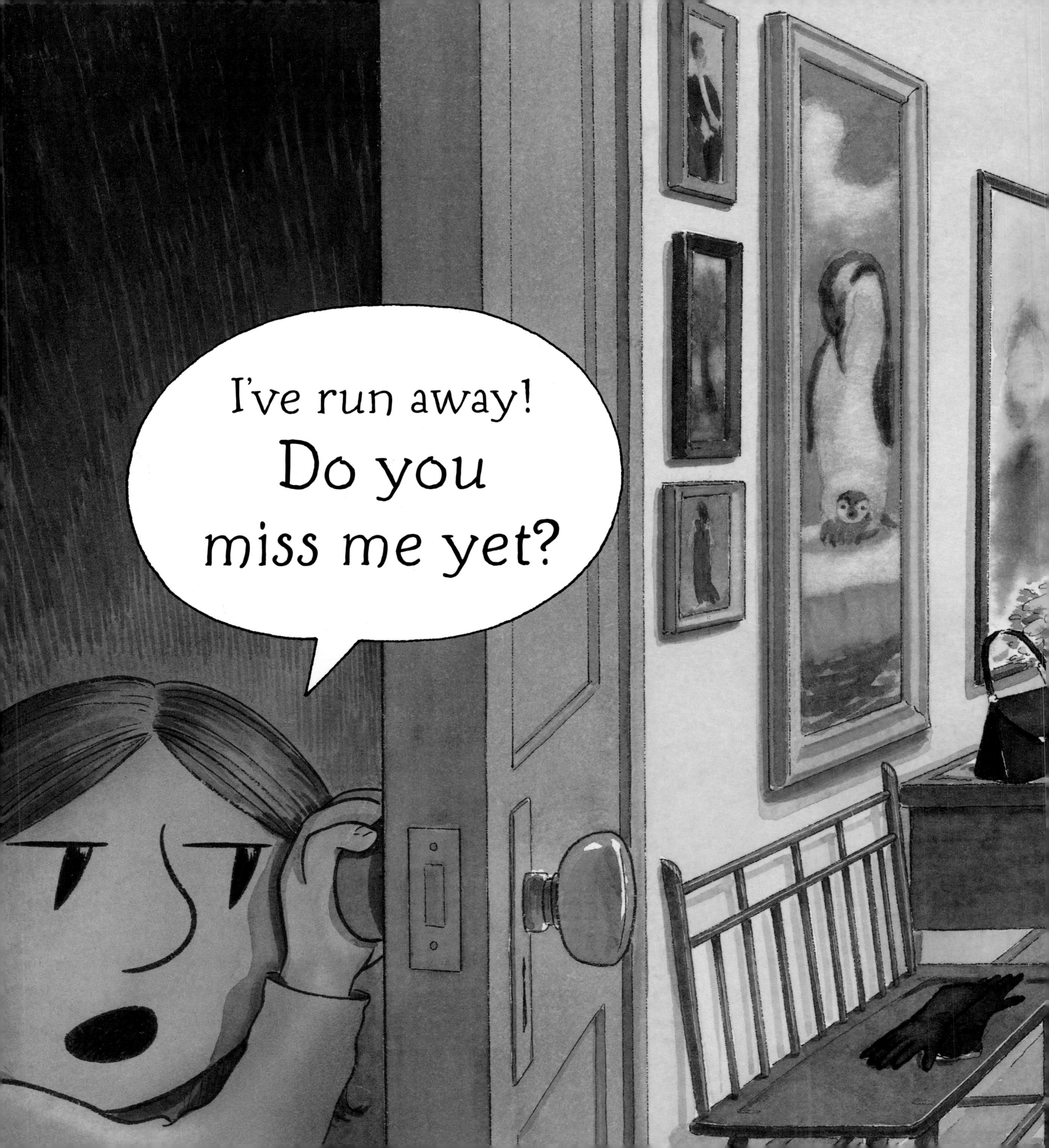
I've run away!
Do you
miss me yet?

We miss you already, Sugar.
Hope you won't be
gone forever!
Please come home soon.

Well, if you go out, then I'll go somewhere — I don't know where — but somewhere very far away. And maybe, just maybe, I'll never ever come back!

The doorbell rang.
I grabbed Panda and ran to my room.

Guess what? Sarah walked into my room.

I do like Sarah. And she's not stupid. She's silly!

Guess what now? It was time for Daddy and Mommy to go.
So I told them three very important things.

And finally, they went out.

After they left, Sarah and I were so busy we didn't have time to go all the way to the South Pole. Sarah heated up cheese pizza, with pepperoni and pineapple on top.

Then we put orange lipstick on our noses, cheeks, and lips. We looked like clowns, and I liked that.

And before I went to bed, Sarah didn't make me
wash off any of my clown makeup. I liked that, too.
And she read me my monster book – five times!
That was so-ooo cool.

Guess what else? This morning, when I tiptoed into Daddy and Mommy's room, there they were — asleep and snoring in the big bed.

I gave them squeezy hugs and noisy kisses — and they both woke up.

And when they saw me, they were so happy I didn't forget to come back — all the way from the South Pole. So I told them three more very important things.

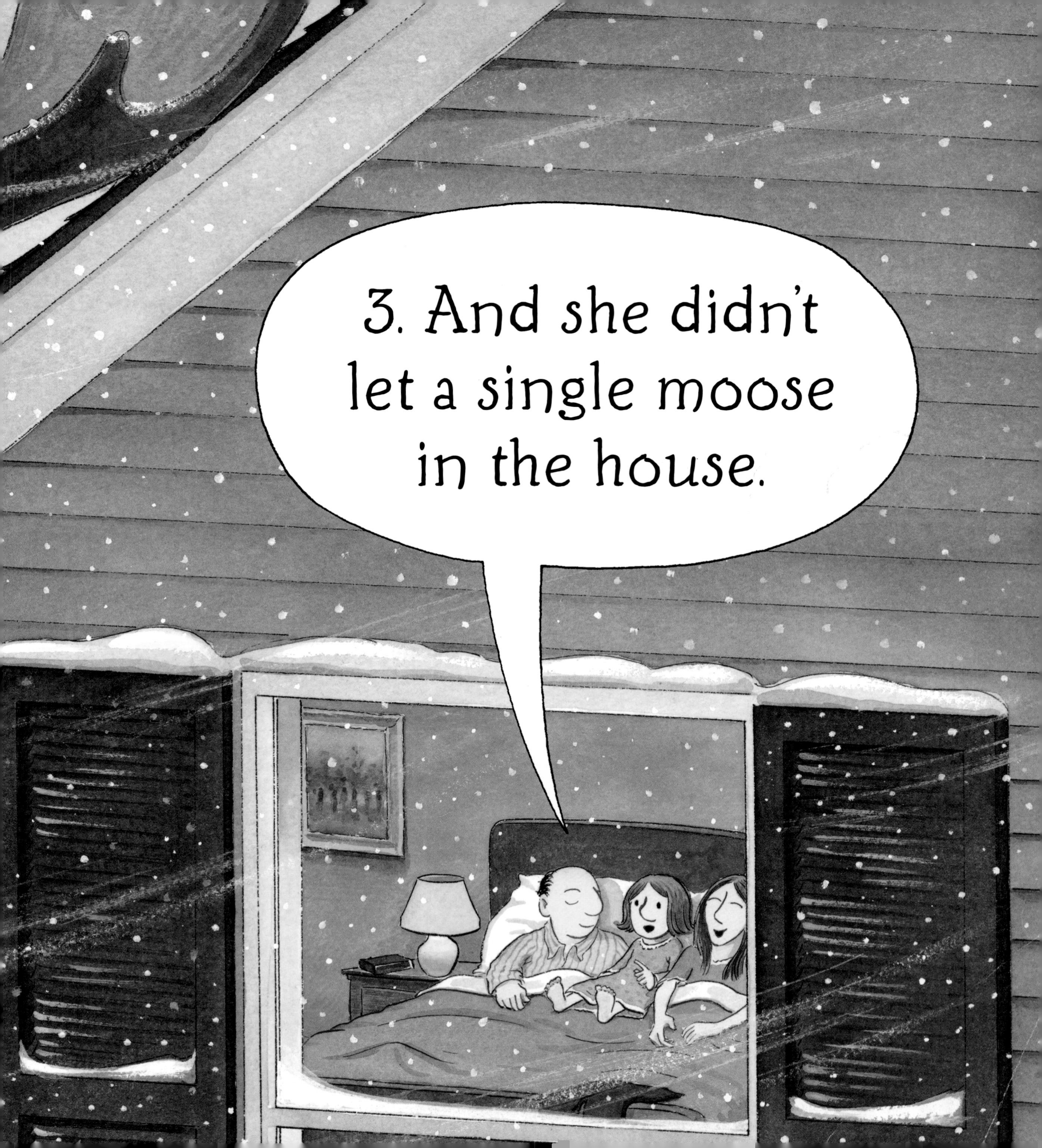
3. And she didn't let a single moose in the house.